This book belongs to:

. . . .

. . . .

. . . .

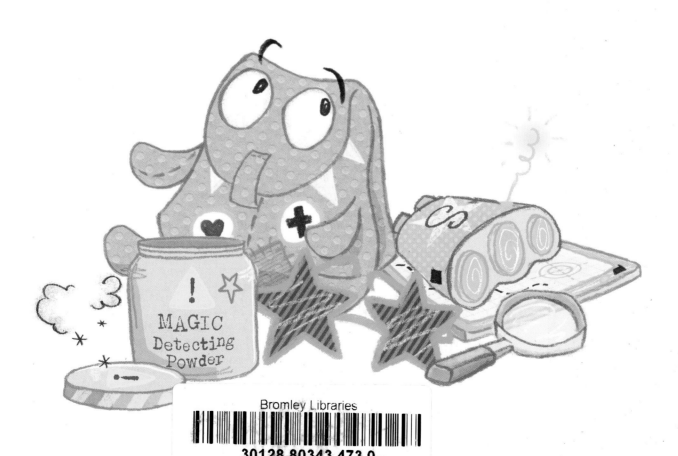

To Elowyn and Pippa - JC

For Lauren from Auntie L x - LS

SKY PRIVATE EYE AND THE CASE OF THE SPARKLY SLIPPER
First published in Great Britain in 2018 by Five Quills
93 Oakwood Court, London W14 8JZ
www.fivequills.co.uk
Five Quills is a trademark of Five Quills

Edited by Natascha Biebow at Blue Elephant Storyshaping
Designed by Jo Spooner

A CIP record for this title is available from the British Library

ISBN 978 0 9935537 2 1

1 3 5 7 9 10 8 6 4 2

Printed in the EU by Pulsio Print

SKY PRIVATE EYE
AND THE CASE OF THE
SPARKLY SLIPPER

Jane Clarke   Loretta Schauer

FIVE
QUILLS

Sky Private Eye was dreaming of cupcakes when the red cherry on the Cupcake Communicator went

beep beep-beep!

It was just past midnight. Sky leapt out of bed.
"Sky Private Eye. Clues and Cupcakes are our speciality," she answered. **"How can we help?"**

It was the Prince, calling from Fairytale Palace.

"I have to give the best costume prize at the Fancy Dress Ball, but the winner's vanished. She left behind a strange, sparkly slipper!"

"Keep calm," Sky told him. "We're on our way!"

"It's a fairytale emergency! Our mission is to find the owner of a mystery slipper," Sky told her dog Snuffle.

They jumped on the scooter, clicked on the Moonbeam headlights and whizzed off through Fairytale Town.

Everyone was in the ballroom.
Sky and Snuffle put on their Star Shades
to examine the sparkly slipper.

"Magic has happened here," Sky said, pulling on her special Magic-Proof Gloves to bag the evidence. Then she turned to the guests.

"I need to interview everyone who saw the girl who was wearing these," she said.

"The **sparkle** was so bright
I couldn't see the girl's face!"
the Big Bad Wolf told Sky.

"She arrived in a **golden coach**,"
said the biggest of the Billy Goats Gruff.

"Pulled by **six white horses**,"
added the smallest of the Three Little Pigs.

"And, just before midnight,
I saw a **Fairy Godmother**
with a wand!" Jack said.

"Magic makes this case extra complicated," Sky told Snuffle.

"But we can solve it with detective skills!"
"How?" asked the Prince.
"Take the slipper back to the shop and dust it for fingerprints,"
said Sky. "And make some cupcakes, of course."

"There are no finger or paw prints on this slipper," Sky sighed.
"Can you detect anything, Snuffle?"
Snuffle sniffed it.

Woof-a-tchoo! he sneezed.

"Never mind," said Sky. "Have a freshly-
made Don't-Be-Disappointed Cupcake!"

Snuffle gobbled it up and wagged his tail.
"Time to find the foot that fits the slipper!"
said Sky Private Eye.

At Bo Peeper's Opticians, Little Bo Peep's foot was **too big**. "Never mind," said Sky. "Have a Don't-Be-Disappointed Cupcake."

At the cottage in the woods,
Little Red Riding Hood's
foot was too small.

"Have a Don't-Be-
Disappointed Cupcake,"
said Sky.

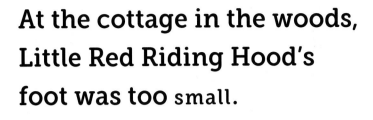

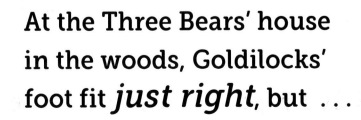

At the Three Bears' house
in the woods, Goldilocks'
foot fit *just right*, but ...

. . . she didn't have the other slipper, so it wasn't her. "Never mind," said Sky. "Have a Don't-Be-Disappointed Cupcake."

There was an excited **woof!** from outside.
The Prince and Sky rushed out to see.
"Clever Snuffle!" said Sky. "**Mouse footprints!**
And look! There are bits of **pumpkin** along this track.
These clues are very odd . . ."

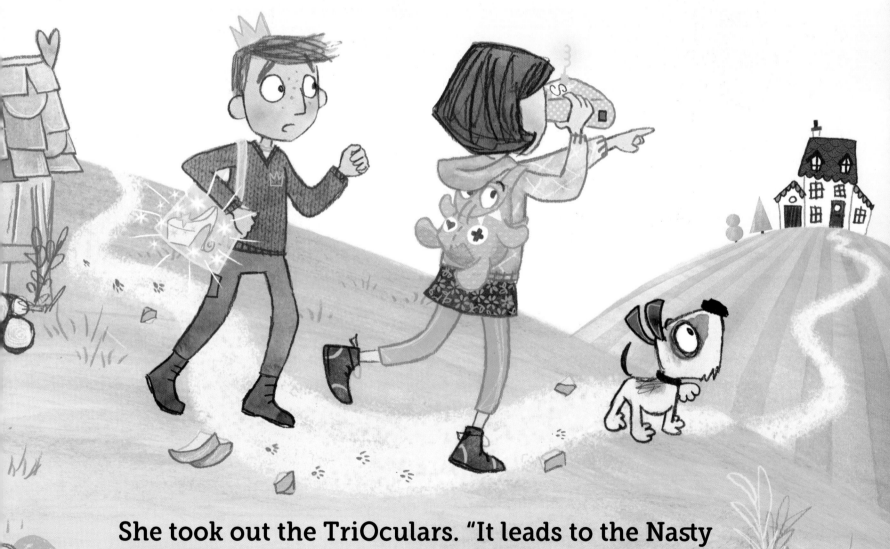

She took out the TriOculars. "It leads to the Nasty
Sisters' house. Let's investigate!"

The elder Nasty Sister crammed the slipper on her foot.

"It fits!" she told the Prince. "I win!"

The younger Nasty Sister grabbed the slipper and squashed her foot into it.

"No, me! I'm the winner!" she cried.

"It doesn't fit right," the Prince sighed.

"These sisters definitely need a cupcake," Sky murmured. But when she opened the box, there were no more Don't-Be-Disappointed Cupcakes left!

Woof! barked Snuffle.

Sky hurried into the Nasty Sisters' pantry to investigate. Their stepsister was hard at work. As she scrubbed, she whispered to her pet mice: "The ball last night was fun! You turned into horses and the pumpkin became a golden coach . . ."

Bucket for Cinders

"Stop her!"

The Nasty Sisters thundered in after Sky.

"Eek, mice!" squealed the sisters.
Sky held out the slipper. "Try this on," she said.

"NO!" shrieked the Nasty Sisters.
"Get back to work, Cinderella!"

"Time to **Bake it Better!**" said Sky, dropping the slipper.

She got out her Carrycake Kit and began to bake cupcakes as fast as she could.

Ping! went the on-the-go oven. Sky pressed the **Quick Cool** button, and stuffed a cupcake into each sister's mouth.

"Yum!" they said, gobbling them up.
"These are my Nice-Not-Nasty Cupcakes," Sky said.
"You'll never be nasty again!"

The Prince held out the slipper for Cinderella to try on.

"It fits!" he cried.

Swooosh!

In a burst of magic, the Fairy Godmother
appeared and waved her wand.

"Cinderella designed all the costumes for the Ball," the Fairy Godmother explained. "She didn't have time to finish hers. I only used magic so she wouldn't miss the Ball. But when the clock struck midnight . . ."

". . . the magic wore off and Cinderella vanished," Sky said. The Fairy Godmother nodded, then she disappeared in a flash.

The Prince knelt down . . .

FLASH

"Cinderella, this key is the prize for the best costume. It's for your own fancy-dress shop. Please make me a different costume for every ball!"

Cinderella beamed. "I've always dreamt of having my own shop!"

Sky baked a special batch of cupcakes for the opening day. All of Fairytale Town was there.

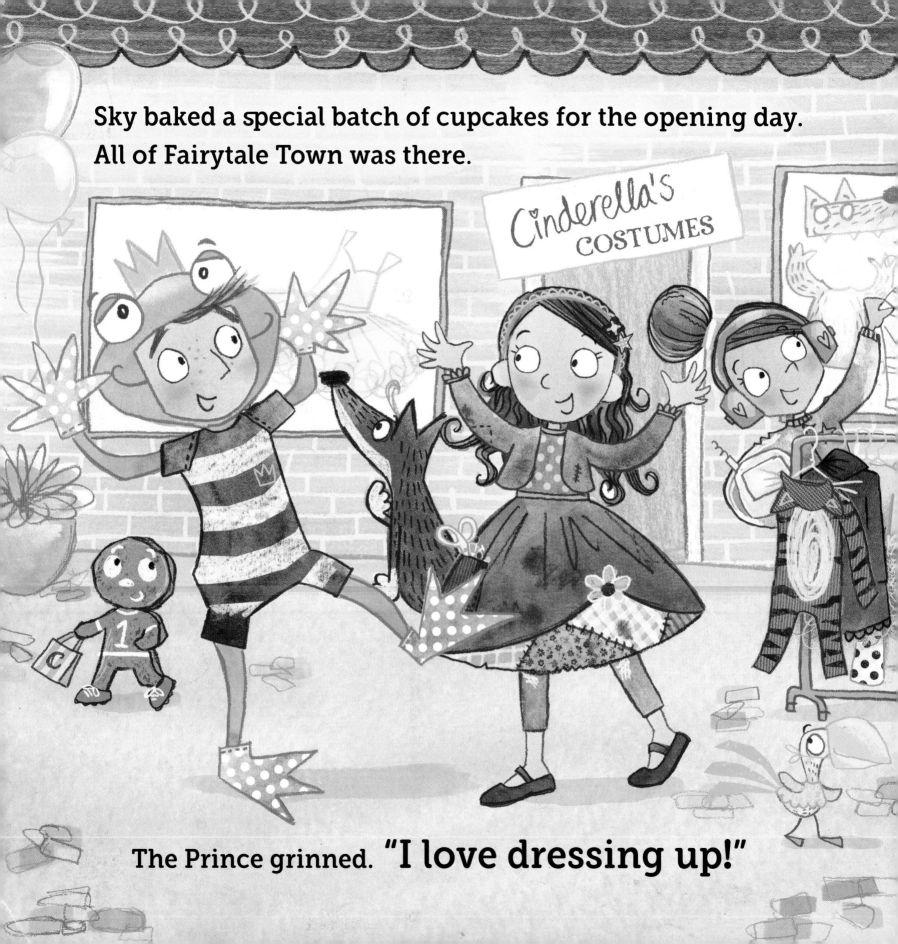

Cinderella's COSTUMES

The Prince grinned. "I love dressing up!"

"Mission accomplished!" Sky giggled.

Woof! barked Snuffle,
balancing a cupcake on his nose.

Sky's Chocolate Cupcakes

Makes 12 Nice-Not-Nasty Cupcakes. Eat one to prevent all sorts of nastiness.

INGREDIENTS

100g flour from Fairytale Mill*
40g cocoa
160g caster sugar from Cinderella's kitchen*
1 ½ teaspoons baking powder
Pinch of salt from the Fairy Godmother*
50g unsalted butter, softened
2 eggs from the Little Red Hen*
150ml milk from Little Boy Blue's cow*
½ teaspoon vanilla extract

Shop-bought ingredients will also work.

For the frosting:
80g unsalted butter, softened
250g icing sugar
25ml milk
¼ teaspoon vanilla extract
Hearts and coloured sprinkles

To make the cupcakes:
1. Ask your grown-up to preheat the oven to 170°C (HOT!)
2. Put on your Bake it Better apron and measure out the ingredients.
3. In a large mixing bowl, use your Stir Crazy spoon to mix the flour, cocoa, caster sugar, baking powder, salt and butter in a bowl. Beat the mixture.
4. Add in the eggs and continue mixing. Slowly add in the milk and vanilla extract.
5. Blend until as smooth as the Prince's new velvet cloak.
6. Place the cupcake cases on a baking tin and fill each 2/3 full with the cupcake mixture.
7. Ask your grown-up to put them in the oven. Bake for 20–25 minutes, (HOT!) until your grown-up sticks in a toothpick and it comes out clean.
8. Ask your grown-up to put the cupcakes out of reach of nasty sisters (and brothers) (HOT!) and let them cool while you make the frosting.

To make the frosting:
9. Beat the softened butter and icing sugar together, then slowly add the milk and vanilla extract. Keep beating until the mixture looks like fluffy white mice.
10. Ice the cupcakes and decorate with hearts and coloured sprinkles.

(HOT!) *You will need an adult to help.*